Fossils at the Cove

📖 Just Right Reader

Rose liked getting a close look at fossils. While at home, she chose a zone on the map to scope out with her pals.

They're going to be stoked!

Rose rode to see her pals, Cole and Slone.

"There is a cave at a cove that's close by!"

Rose noted the kind of fossils they could find.

"I hope we find all of those fossils!" said Slone.

Rose, Cole, and Slone rode their bikes to the cove.

Before they went into the cave, Rose got out the rope and stakes from her bag.

"They'll help us find our way out, so we can go back home," said Rose.

Slone and Cole were close while Rose put the rope in the holes.

Rose saw lots of stones and spoke to Slone and Cole.

"I suppose this is a good spot to stop."

Cole made jokes as he placed cones to track the spots they'd checked. Slone picked up many stones and hoped to expose a fossil, but no luck.

Rose got a big rock. She poked and whacked it until it broke.

Once the rock broke open, a fossil was exposed!

The kids froze. They all spoke out at once.

"A trilobite!"

"I hope my dad will be home to see this!" said Rose.

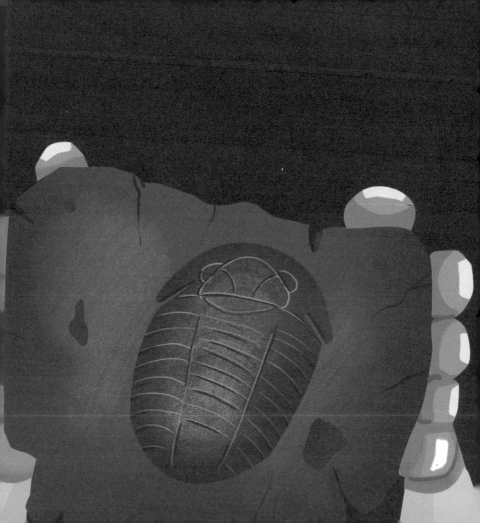

When Rose got home, Dad saw the trilobite in the stone.

"Amazing! You know, I think you'll travel to many places on the globe and find a whole lot of fossils."

"I hope I find lots of bones!" said Rose.

Phonics Fun

- Write the CVC word.
- Add a final e to the CVC word.
- Read the new word.

| cap | cub | rod |
| not | tub | |

Comprehension

Did this book make you think of another book? Which one and why?

High Frequency Words

once   out

Decodable Words

bone	note
broke	poke
chose	rode
close	rope
Cole	Rose
cone	Slone
cove	scope
expose	spoke
froze	stoke
globe	stone
hole	suppose
home	those
hope	zone
joke	